CIP Data is available.
Published in the United States 2005 by
Blue Apple Books
515 Valley Street, Maplewood, N.J. 07040
www.blueapplebooks.com
Distributed in the U.S. by Chronicle Books

First Edition
Printed in China
ISBN: 1-59354-089-2
1 3 5 7 9 10 8 6 4 2

william
and
The Dragon

by Harriet Ziefert
Pictures by Richard Brown

 **Blue Apple Books**

"Six o'clock,"
said the watchman of Pell.
"Six o'clock," said the watchman,
"and all is not well."

People came running
to the center of Pell.

"Why has the watchman
started to yell?"

The mayor stood tall
and said with a frown,
"Whatever you are,
you must leave this town!"

The mayor called the fire chief.
"Bring your red truck.
We'll show this monster
he's run out of luck."

Fire Chief Charlie
did not miss a beat.
He unrolled two hoses and
sprayed water on its feet.

The beast liked water.
He wanted a drink.

"A big, thirsty monster . . .
we'll have to rethink."

"Go away," said the mayor.
"Little boy, you're a pest.
I'll take care of the dragon.
I know what's best."

Said the mayor to the dragon,
"You must go away!
I order you gone
by the end of the day!"

The dragon got mad.
He stomped his big feet.
Said the butcher, "I think
he wants something to eat!"

Now came the police with
their booming machine.
With everyone gathered,
it was quite a scene.

The police shouted orders.
"Cover your ears!"
They hadn't used the machine
for seventeen years.

The dragon sneezed
when the noise was done.
He wasn't scared and
he didn't run.

William was small.
William was smart.
He was sure the dragon
had a kind heart.

The dragon looked down
and said with a smile,
"I just wanted to visit
your town for a while."

"I'm from a faraway place.
It's called Kung Fooey.
Everyone calls me
Alexander Ahh Chooey."

William and Chooey—
they walked down the street.

William waved good-bye
and planned when they'd meet.